MYRTLE
AND
CHUCK

A Story for Children of All Ages

by
Gary E. Sabbag

AuthorHouse™
1663 Liberty Drive
Bloomington, IN 47403
www.authorhouse.com
Phone: 833-262-8899

Because of the dynamic nature of the Internet, any web addresses or links contained in this book may have changed
since publication and may no longer be valid. The views expressed in this work are solely those of the author and do
not necessarily reflect the views of the publisher, and the publisher hereby disclaims any responsibility for them.

Any people depicted in stock imagery provided by Getty Images are models,
and such images are being used for illustrative purposes only.
Certain stock imagery © Getty Images.

This book is printed on acid-free paper.

ISBN: 978-1-6655-0502-4 (sc)
978-1-6655-0504-8 (hc)
978-1-6655-0503-1 (e)

Library of Congress Control Number: 2020920742

Print information available on the last page.

Published by AuthorHouse 01/23/2021

authorHOUSE®

MYRTLE
AND
CHUCK

A Story for Children of All Ages

By:
Gary E. Sabbag

Illustrated by:
Larry J. Walker

MYRTLE
AND
CHUCK

By:
Gary E. Sabbag

Illustrated by:
Larry J. Walker

_____

Dedicated to

Lol,

the original Myrtle.

_____

Chapter I: **Slow and Fast**

Once upon a pond,
in clime tropic and 'yond,
there lived a turtle,

named Myrtle,

and a duck,

named Chuck.

The pond upon which these two did live—
     in, around, under and upon, to say rather—
had a legendary narrative.
     From word of mouth, beak and bill it foregathered.

Being that
        a large rock sat
                in the middle of this little loch,
the pond was known,
        not as Stone,
                but appropriately as Rock.

Rock Pond

Rock Pond, like any place in the wild,
        be it land, sea, air or this small body of water,
was no place for a child.
        T'was the scene of natural, perpetual slaughter.

Rock Pond was as vicious as a small jungle.
Life was lost easily by one small bungle.

Big things fed on little things,
    little things on small.
Big teeth snapped at flying wings.
    Ants made plants fall.

Every living thing sings its song—
    some are short; some are long.
Some fast or slow, some weak or strong—
    but never, never is anyone's song wrong.

And so it was with Myrtle and Chuck,
    two very different breeds, indeed.
They were contrary as . . . well . . . turtle and duck,
    when came time for them to proceed.

Myrtle was always sure and slow.
    Chuck did things speedy and fast.

Each did the best they knew, though.
    One can only use what one hast.

Differences abounded between these two.
The following is a list of only a few:

Myrtle was reptile;
    Chuck a bird.
Myrtle was docile;
    Chuck was always heard.

Myrtle nested in the sand.
    Chuck nested in the trees.
She made sure all was planned.
    He did things on sprees.

Upon her back she wore a shell.
Feathers for Chuck served him quite well.

Myrtle could go for months without eating.
Fullness for Chuck was always fleeting.

Myrtle's life expectancy was long;
    his rather short.
Chuck could fly high and strong.
    She was an earthbound, self-contained fort.

Yes, they were different, there's no doubt;
but similarities abounded, if one just looked about.
Actually, they had more in common than they knew.
The following is a list of only a few:

Swimming was natural to both.
Each was in the middle of growth.

Soon both would hatch their young,
so close by their nests they hung.

Each had four healthy eggs to tend.
And these they'd defend to the very end.

Each had a mate who'd recently died.
Both were so sad, they tearfully cried.
But still, their nests they faithfully attended,
all the while needing to be befriended.

On and on they worked hard as a drone,
feeling half-empty and very much alone.

Except for a narrow-minded streak,
the mind of each was clearly not weak.
At each other they'd sometimes sneak a peek,
and often expound with the same old critique.

"That turtle's so slow!" Chuck would say,
"She creeps and crawls every which way.
How silly are the things she does.
She's as slow as molasses ever was.

"Whenever she leaves her nest to go somewhere,
by the time she arrives, it's time to leave there.

"She never gets a single thing done.
I like to watch her just for fun.

"Amazing she ever finished her nest in the sand,
at such a slow pace—one I could never stand.

"One day she stopped for the longest time.
        I thought she'd finished with her life.
But once again, she began her strange pantomime,
        slowly dragging herself along with strife.

"She's got to be the slowest thing in the universe.
If she moved much slower, she'd be going in reverse!"

And then Myrtle would think, quite aghast:
"That crazy duck is much too fast!

"How silly are the things he does,
frazzling feathers into so much fuzz,
then zipping around all the day through,
forgetting where he's come from or going to.

"He'll leave his nest time after time;
        but never stop and think ahead.
Always working himself overtime,
        one of these days he'll end up dead.

"It's a wonder he ever finished his aerie,
        up there in the hole in the tree.
Such hustle and bustle
                and wasted use of muscle–
                        where does he get all his energy?

"It seems he doesn't even know
that he's so fast he's really slow!"

Neither knew the other well,
        nor took the time to know
uses of feather or shell;
        advantage fast or slow.

It's not that one disliked the other;
each took one look, but not another.
They remained within a self-made cell,
living their lives in parallel.

They'd never tried mere close contact.
Coexistence was a matter of fact.
But, whene'er it came to the prized Rock,
against each other's head they'd knock.

Chapter II: **The Legend of the Rock**

The rock, from which Rock Pond got its name,
> protruded up from the middle of the pond.
All inhabitants knew its fame.
> Of the legend and the rock, all were fond.

The story that had grown up in this place
> said: "Whoever shall sit upon this rock
will be free from the eternal chase,
> free from the troubles of the flock."

So rock sitters could enjoy some peace,
> as long as they stayed sitting there,
which usually was 'til the light of day ceased.
> After that, the sitter better beware.

Some rock sitters, who tried to stay all night,
> mysteriously disappeared, before morning's light.
Accusers of Big Alice, the alligator, were right.
> Her loud burps were proof—and quite impolite.

The origins of the Legend of the Rock
> arose a long, long time ago.
Earth was brand-new and still in shock.
> The planet was just beginning to grow.

Nature stretched and yawned from its very source.
> Earth emerged and began to awake.
Volcanoes erupted with great force.
> All would quake, shake and break.

First, t'was only a well and a fountain.
> Then up a very large rock pushed.
Actually the tip of an underground mountain,
> instantly, Rock Pond formed with a: "Swoosht"!

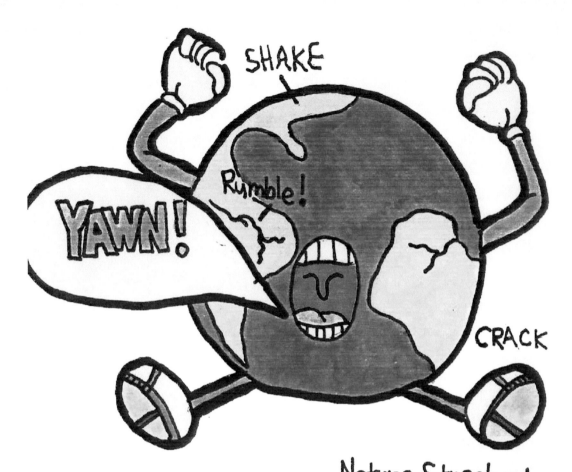

Nature Streched
and YAWNED!

One day a prehistoric mouse
    decided to make his way to the rock.
He wanted it as his fun-house.
    He frolicked all over that block.

Then along came a Tyrannosaurus Rex,
a huge dinosaur one should not vex.

He told the mouse,
    with a roar that could bend steel:
"Get off, you louse.
    I want to rest my sore heel!"

But bravely the mouse stood on the rock.
    He'd worked too hard to attain this spot.
He'd floated there on a shamrock,
    and give it up, he would not.

The dinosaur raised his big foot that ached,
  and was about to squash the mouse where he stood.
But suddenly, the earth trembled and quaked,
  removing the dinosaur from the rock's neighborhood.

A large crevice opened up.
  Down the slope of the underground mountain he fell.
Earth gave a loud: "Hiccup!"
  And the Tyrannosaurus Rex drowned in the deep, deep well.

From then on, to this very day,
  anyone upon the rock may stay.
And enjoy a pleasant holiday,
  free of being fearful prey.
    Or so it would seem that way...

The Dinosaur
Raised his BIG Foot

Chapter III: **Race for the Rock**

As it always was at Rock Pond,
    this was the start of a busy day.
Creatures hurried, scurried to abscond,
    working in their usual way.

"Living things gathered, stored, and nursed."

Even before the morn's sunburst,
    living things gathered, stored and nursed.
All had a mighty, powerful thirst:
    to get out onto the sacred rock first.

Everyone was in on the daily race.
    All wanted to sit in that hallowed place.
On the rock they were free from the life-death chase.
    There they rose above the commonplace.

Myrtle, the turtle, and Chuck, the duck,
    seemed the most likely contestants that day.
One of them, with a little bit of luck,
    upon the prized rock would lay.

But there were others, too, involved in this race—
    unscrupulous characters, who hid their face.
Though the rock is a fairly safe place,
    it's dangerous getting to that base.

En route, one could be attacked–
      that rock a large crowd will attract.
Or, while there one's home could be ransacked–
      a real possibility, not abstract.

Three main culprits get special heed:
      Big Alice, the alligator, and her little son Fred,
plus Stella, the stealing starling, of robber breed.
      All three are a terrible dread.

Little Fred, Big Alice's spoiled son,
was thought a brat by everyone.
He'd tease or seize and do as he'd please,
while his mother's protection would never cease.

Stella was lazy as the day is long.
      She worked hardest at shirking work.
She'd take things to which she didn't belong.
      All day at the pond she'd sit and lurk.

Now, Myrtle's eggs were buried in the sand.
All else too, was thoroughly planned.
Soon her babies would be ready to hatch,
and all her free time they would soon snatch.

And Chuck's eggs, too, were ready to crack.
And soon free time he'd also lack.

So, get away now and enjoy was their plan:
"Go sit on the rock, while you still can!"

Because of the legend, the first one there,
put in the heart of the others an awful scare.
No one dared challenge the right to sit.
That's how much power this rock could emit.

So Myrtle methodically made ready to go.
She set off for the rock, steady and slow.
Chuck, in his nest in the hole in the tree,
prepared, in a rush, facsimilarly.

Fred and Stella watched over this scene.
Would they get their chance, today, to be mean?

Myrtle waddled to the water's edge:
  "I'll be the first one today," she vowed.
She moved deliberately, without hedge.
  All superfluous thoughts she disallowed.

By being ahead even just one move,
she made her progress greatly improve.
Chuck—quite the opposite—on the other hand,
did things swiftly and never planned.

Myrtle always stayed busy in her mind.
Chuck's busy-ness was of a different kind.
His method was impulse and quickness.
It seemed he had some lunatic-ness.

He always knew what had to be done,
  but he did things so fast and on the run,
that his comings and goings got terribly spun,
  and he had to go back to where he'd begun.

He was so fast, he really was slow.
  She was so slow, she really was fast.
True to their species— status quo,
  these two were such a contrast.

Myrtle cautiously slipped into the pond.
  She started swimming for the rock.
And how, upon seeing this, did Chuck respond?
  He went into utter shock!

Out of the hole in the tree, he peeked.
Seeing Myrtle's progress, he gasped and eeked!
Bolting onto the branch quickly, he streaked.
He took to the air, and again he shrieked.

He went a ways, then returned to his nest.
Frantically he plucked feathers from his breast,
covered his eggs so that cold would be less,
then, once again, took to the air with stress.

Again, he made a volte-face,
and went back to his home base.
He forgot to cover the hole in the tree.
And he wanted the eggs safe as could be.

Now checking, assuring there wasn't a trace,
hurriedly putting the last twig in place,
he at last took flight, flapping his best,
all ready to resume his cherished quest.

Meanwhile, Myrtle chose cautiously to proceed,
all the time watching Alice and Fred feed
on some poor unrecognizable breed.
"That's how it goes at Rock Pond, indeed.

"And I wonder what's become of that robber bird?
From that stealing starling I've not heard a word.
Ah, there, she's just stolen her lunch.
Yup," said Myrtle, "that was my hunch."

But on toward the rock, her goal,
she carried on her careful stroll.
Meanwhile, Chuck was flying furiously fast.
Speedily by Myrtle he'd soon zoom past.

But just then, Chuck realized that in his haste,
        he'd forgotten to eat: "Oh, what a waste!
If I don't eat now and on the rock become placed,
        it'll be all day 'til food again I taste."

So change his course Chuck once again did.
Diving into a patch of duckweed, he made his bid.
Gulping down what was weed, now mash,
he got away again in a flurried flash.

Beating his wings hard, he swooped down.
But quickly he had to pull up with a frown.
Myrtle was just then climbing onto the rock.
The food in Chuck's stomach felt like a clump of chalk.

Feeling ill, he flew back to his nest.
He hung his head and upchucked on his chest.

All that day Myrtle warmed in the sun.
    She certainly was the envy of everyone.
She was having herself a great deal of fun;
    and this she did 'til day was done.

Before dark, she returned to her nest,
happy to have had a peaceful rest.

But resting was the last thing on Chuck's mind.
    "Tomorrow," he swore, "I won't be left behind!"
What did early morn's light find?
    Chuck busily bustling, bill to grind.

Chapter IV: **Rematch**

Chuck was determined to get to the rock first.
He stayed up all the night through.
His routine by now was well rehearsed,
as he prepared for his rock rendezvous.

By early light,
Chuck was a sight:
frazzled, razzled and pooped.

But bravely he forged on,
'til the break of dawn:
he swooped, looped and drooped.

He was as tired as tired could be,
leaving his tree finally.
He'd done all he thought he could.

He'd feathered his nest;
done all the rest.
Yet he hadn't done all he should.

He hadn't covered the hole in the tree.
It was left uncovered completely.
Getting to the rock first made him blind.
This and nothing else was on his mind.

And besides, so exhausted was he,
hardly could he fly—let alone see.

So when he tried to land on the rock,
into it he crashed with a: "Squawk!"

What a sudden, abrupt stop!
Into the water he dropped.
He trudged his way to the top.
Once there, he fainted and flopped.

Chapter V: To the Rescue! To the Rescue!

Myrtle'd seen Chuck, and thought: "How silly!"
So did two frogs on a water lily.
All of the pond's creatures had seen, in fact.
That type of spectacle, attention does attract.

"Knee-deep, knee-deep,"
      loud and clear croaked one frog.
"Knee-deep, knee-deep,"
      continued the dialogue.

As both frogs measured the depth of pond where they stood,
Big Alice appeared and chewed them up: "Goooooood!"

Alice's son, Fred, tried to catch fish.
Much too fast, they escaped with a: "Swish!"

And with Stella the stealing starling,
      all of this did not slip by.
She sat on a branch in a tree snarling,
      peering down over all like a spy.

Whenever she was nigh,
Myrtle kept a keen eye.

She saw Stella look at Chuck, then his nest.
Wasn't hard to guess the rest.
She knew Stella'd be up to no good.
Myrtle vowed she'd do all she could.

Myrtle thought: "Should I try to wake the duck?
      I could walk over to his tree.
Perhaps I could scare the bird with some luck.
      I'll just go over there and see."

"Myrtle saw Stella
look at Chuck, then
his NEST."

So slowly and steadily she started toward Chuck's tree.
Not losing a second, she left immediately.

As Myrtle advanced, she thought all the time,
of what to do next to prevent this crime.
Stretching out her neck as far as it'd go,
she wondered: "What to do there, I want to know?

"Perhaps I'll shake a bush or small tree.
        That could attract the duck's attention.
Hope he'll awake in time to see,
        the starling's bad intention."

Stella didn't even notice Myrtle,
        besides, that wouldn't have stopped her.
On the ground what harm is a turtle?
        Myrtle'd really need a helicopter.

Myrtle silently coaxed, as she planned her advance:
"C'mon duck, hurry! Snap out of your trance!"

Taking one last glance–
      Chuck out like a light–
Stella saw her chance,
      and she took to flight.

She landed on the branch beside the hole in the tree.
Stealing a look inside, she found it hard to see.
She couldn't discern what was inside.
Into the darkness she peered and spied.

"Yes, there's something there!
      At least I think I'm right.
But, better take care
      and bring it into the light."

So she pulled on the nest.
      But it was too big for the hole.
"It's full! I'm blessed!"
      she exclaimed as she stole.

Myrtle had just arrived under the tree,
as Stella was shouting out her glee.

Stella tugged to see what's to eat.
      All of a sudden, out the nest popped!
Stella was knocked off her feet,
      while gently to the ground the nest dropped.

Right in front of Myrtle the nest went: "Plop!"
Very casually she walked up on top.
Then she pulled in arms, legs and tail,
and made herself ready to all avail.

Her shell perfectly covered the whole nest.
Now she'd wait and let Stella do the rest.

Back up in the tree,
Stella looked around to see
if what she'd done had been seen.
All appeared to be serene.

So she dove to the ground, on the scene.
When she arrived her shout was obscene:

"Eek! What is this turtle doing here?
        Come on, you, get up, get off of there!
From where did you suddenly appear?
        These eggs are mine! Can't you hear?"

Thus on and on and on Stella jeered.
Out from her shell Myrtle only leered.

She thought: "With Stella's loud protest,
surely the duck will start an inquest."

And sure enough, the noise caused such unrest,
        that from out his deep sleep Chuck was wrest.
Raising his head he asked: "Who's the pest?"
        Then saw the commotion involving his nest.

Instantly into the air Chuck flew,
soaring on high to get a better view.
There below he heard and saw
Stella yelling: "Caw-caw! Caw-caw!"

He saw Myrtle defending his nest with a: "Hiss!"
Chuck, stunned, asked: "For me she does this?"

He was about to lend his help forthright,
    when, to one side, he caught a terrible sight.
For a second he was frozen with fright.
    Fred was taking advantage of the fight.

"Why's this guy there sneaking around?
Seems the turtle's nest he found.
While the turtle's holding up well,
this little lizard, I'll dispel.

"This calls for fast action," Chuck said.
And he dove down directly on little Fred.

Chuck grabbed Fred in his bill by a hind leg,
just before Fred was about to eat an egg.

Fred was stopped suddenly, unaware,
biting into nothing but thin air.

Then Chuck took off to try to help Myrtle–
     while Fred dangled from his bill upside-down.
Stella was pecking the shell of the turtle.
     "Bombs away!" Chuck cried, letting Fred fall to the ground.

Down toward Stella Fred sped.
Both sprawled, heel-over-head.
And when they came up-side right,
Fred's teeth clamped Stella's tail tight.

Though Stella screamed like a quail,
Fred would not let loose her tail.
So, then she tried to take to flight,
but Fred held on with vice-grip bite.

Stella could barely get off the ground.
Myrtle and Chuck laughed and rolled around.
Both of them heartily approved:
two less problems—justly removed.

Soon Big Alice took up the chase,
        while Stella said a prayer verse.
Trying to keep with the chaotic pace,
        Big Alice yelled a harsh curse.

Big Alice took up the CHASE

This could have gone on all day,
these three carrying on in this way,
but finally Stella's tail feathers did fail,
and Fred fell to Earth with a resounding wail.

None seemed the worse for wear.
Fred was bruised here and there.

Big Alice felt it too much to bear.
And Stella, feathers light, had quite a scare.

While Stella just barely escaped,
into each other's face Myrtle and Chuck gaped.
Their eyes shone a bit more wise.
Thanks and respect seemed to materialize.

Suddenly, there came a peeping.
        And when Myrtle climbed off Chuck's nest,
there sat four ducklings squeaking,
        singing out their hungry request.

Chuck was struck with marvel and wonder.
Immediately he sought food o'er and under.

Hopefully Myrtle returned to her brood,
arriving in time to see babies exude.
She was filled with happiness and joy,
as she caressed her three girls and one boy.

On one of his frantic passes by,
     in his search for food for his demanding brood,
Chuck came down out of the sky.
     He and Myrtle expressed mutual gratitude.

Chuck unfurled his wing of blue, green and red,
     and laid it gently upon Myrtle's head.
"We shall be friends until we are dead,"
     both vowed in loving words unsaid.

Chapter VI: A New Generation

Rock Pond's world is as before.
Life and the rock will be evermore.

But occasionally an unusual sight can be seen,
that is, to the eye most keen.

Out in the middle of Rock Pond,
        splashing, frolicking with one another,
forming a very special bond,
        ducklings and turtlettes play like sister and brother.

And on the rock, basking in the sun,
        right out in front of everyone,
                peacefully sit a turtle and duck.
                        Naturally, 'tis Myrtle and Chuck.

-THE BEGINNING-

Glossary

abounded: plentiful, in abundance

abscond: to escape, to hide

abstract: general, not exact, not concrete

aerie: lofty nest

avail: help, advantage

basking: enjoying pleasant warmth, lying in or enjoying

befriended: made friends with

bid: an effort to win or attain

breed: a sort or kind (of animal)

brood: offspring; young

bungle: awkward or clumsy job

clime: country, climate or region

coax: to persuade

commotion: disturbance, disorder, confusion, excitement

contrast: opposite, dissimilar, unlike

crevice: small crack

critique: judgment or review

determined: decided, focused, headstrong

dialogue: conversation

discern: to perceive; recognize.

dispel: to drive away, to break up

docile: gentle, easy-going

drone: a worker bee

en route:	on the way
envy:	jealousy
exhausted:	weakened, tired out
exude:	to come forth gradually
facsimilarly:	(made-up word) like a facsimile—meaning copy, duplicate
fond:	feel affection for
foregathered:	to come together; assemble
forged:	moved forward steadily
forthright:	plain, direct
frolicked:	played
gaped:	stared, looked at with surprise
hast:	old-fashioned way to say "have"
haste:	hurry, speed
hunch:	guess
inquest:	investigation
jeered:	rudely shouted, made fun of
keen:	sharp, clever
leered:	looked in a mean way
loch:	lake, body of water
lunatic-ness:	(made-up word) craziness
nigh:	old-fashioned way to say "near", "close by"
obscene:	rude
o'er:	a poetic way to say "over"
origins:	source, beginning
pantomime:	silent actions, gestures

parallel:	traveling along the same lines but not meeting
pledge:	promise
prehistoric:	before written history; about a long, long, long time ago
prey:	one animal that is food for another
protruded:	stuck out from
quest:	adventure, goal; to search for
ransacked:	roughly examined; searched through
rehearsed:	practiced, prepared
rendezvous:	meeting, meeting place
reptile:	cold-blooded, air-breathing animal
resounding:	loud, echoing
rid:	freed from; to eliminate
shamrock:	three- or four-leafed clover; symbolizes good luck
shirking:	avoiding doing something; irresponsible
sprawling:	spread out or extended awkwardly
sprees:	whimsical, wildly amusing outings
status quo:	maintain the current condition or state
strife:	hardship or fighting
trance:	dreamlike state between sleeping and waking
unrecognizable:	impossible to identify
volte-face:	turn about in opposite direction
vowed:	promised
wrest:	to pull away or take from by force
'yond:	beyond, distant

Gary E. Sabbag is a free-lance writer who grew up in the State
of Confusion but now lives in the State of New Hampshire.
Check out his website at "**www.garyesabbagwriter.com**".

Testimonials
(unsolicited) from young readers/listeners:

Dear Mr. Sabbag:
Thank you for telling (reading) us your story. It was great.
My favorite character is Myrtle the turtle.
Thanks.
Your friend,
Willy (Age 8; Tucson, Arizona)

It was funny...
Your friend,
Kristen (Age 8; Tucson, Arizona)

I liked the whole story. ...the animals were funny and nice... I think your story will be a great sucsess (success). I bett (bet) some day you will be a famos (famous) author because you wrote Myrtle and Chucks (Chuck's) adventure.
Robert (Age 9; Miami, Florida)

The part I liked was the chase and the fight. I also liked the way it rymed (rhymed)... I think the begining (beginning) at the end ment (meant) it was the begining (beginning) of (Myrtle and Chuck) being friends.
Natalie (Age 8; Miami, Florida)

I don't think I have heard or read a better childrens (children's) story...
Megan (Age 8; Miami, Florida)

I think that the story was ...entaing (entertaining), real aventure (adventure) and good words...
Natasha (Age 8; Miami, Florida)

I liked how Mertle (Myrtle) dose (does) the opisite (opposite) of Chuck becoause (because) Chuck dose (does) things fast a (and) Merttle dose (does) things slowe (slow).
Emanuel (Age 8; Miami, Florida)

Printed in the United States
By Bookmasters